# MEAN, GREEN, MYSTERY MACHINE

## Written by James Gelsey

SCHOLASTIC INC.

New York  Toronto  London  Auckland  Sydney
Mexico City  New Delhi  Hong Kong  Buenos Aires

ISBN 0-439-55711-9

Copyright © 2003 by Hanna-Barbera.
SCOOBY-DOO and all related characters and elements
are trademarks of and © Hanna-Barbera.
(s03)
Published by Scholastic Inc. All rights reserved.
SCHOLASTIC and associated logos are trademarks and/or
registered trademarks of Scholastic Inc.

Designed by Maria Stasavage

12 11 10 9 8 7 6 5 4 3 2 1                                      3 4 5 6 7 8/0

Special thanks to Duendes del Sur
for cover and interior illustrations.

Printed in the U.S.A.
First printing, November 2003

## Chapter 1

Shaggy and Scooby-Doo were walking home from the movies. The Mystery Machine rolled up along next to them.

"Hey, the Mystery Machine!" Shaggy said. "I guess good old Fred will give us a ride home."

But the van didn't stop. Shaggy and Scooby peeked inside.

"Zoinks! There is no Fred!" Shaggy cried. "In fact, there's no driver!"

A strange greenish glow came from beneath the van. Weird music began to play.

"Ruh-roh," said Scooby.

Then the Mystery Machine started driving — right at them! The two friends dived out of the way. The van kept going and disappeared into the night.

Shaggy and Scooby got up and ran as fast as they could. They burst into a coffeehouse nearby. It was where Fred, Daphne, and Velma liked to hang out.

"Like, the Mystery Machine!" Shaggy cried. "It's after us!"

"Maybe I left the parking brake off," Fred said with a shrug.

"Parking brake?" Shaggy asked.

"No way. That thing was alive.
There was this creepy green glow.
And scary music."

Shaggy and Scooby-Doo dragged
the others outside to see the van.
They found it where Fred had parked
it. There was no sign it had moved.

"Come on, everyone," Fred said.
"It's getting late. Let's head home."

The gang got into the Mystery Machine and started off down the street. They followed a long road up a mountain.

Suddenly, Fred said, "Hey, the steering wheel won't turn!"

The Mystery Machine began to go faster. It drove all over the road.

"Hit the brakes, Freddy!" Daphne cried.

Fred pressed the brake, but nothing happened.

"Zoinks!" Shaggy shouted. "Look!"

He pointed to a sign up ahead. "Road Closed," it said. There was a big cement wall behind it.

Fred pushed a button and a giant parachute shot out from be-

hind the van. It stopped the van
inches from the sign. The gang
sighed in relief.

"Didn't the Mystery Machine
just have a tune-up, Freddy?"
asked Daphne.

"It sure did," Fred said. "First
thing in the morning, we'll go see
Murph the mechanic again."

**Chapter 2**

The next day, the gang visited Murph's Custom Car Shop.

"Sorry, but when your van left here, it was perfect," Murph said. "I checked the brakes twice. They were fine."

"They weren't fine last night," Daphne said.

"Tell you what I'll do," Murph said. "The Mystery Machine is getting up there in miles. I'll give you $5,000 for it."

"What would we do without the Mystery Machine?" asked Daphne.

Scooby looked out the window. He saw the Mystery Machine's greenish glow again. Suddenly, the van drove off — all by itself.

"Rystery Rachine!" he called.

Everyone ran outside. Fred looked down and saw a trail of oil drops.

"Luckily for us, the Mystery Machine is leaking oil," he said.

Scooby put his nose to the ground and sniffed along the trail of oil. The gang followed. The trail came to an end in front of a house. The gang knocked at the front door, and a thin woman opened it.

"Well, I'm always happy to talk
to reporters," she said. "But I'm
right in the middle of a piano les-
son. Come on in and wait in there."

"Uh . . . okay," Velma said.

The gang walked inside. They
saw a young girl sitting at a piano.

"The piano is just a little out of
tune," the woman told the gang.

Scooby and the gang walked into the living room and looked around. There were pictures of a young boy and girl everywhere. There were photos, magazine covers, posters, and even CD covers.

"Hey, like, these are the Mystery Kids!" Shaggy said.

"They sure were popular," Daphne said.

"And they're going to be again!" the woman said.

"You must be the Mystery Kids' biggest fan," Fred said.

"I'm not a fan, I'm their mother!" the woman smiled. "I'm Susan Dinwiddie, and I'm very busy. This interview can't take too long."

Velma explained that they were not reporters. She told Susan that they were looking for their van, the Mystery Machine.

"You own the Mystery Machine?" Susan said. "That was our tour bus. Since they were the Mystery Kids, we called the van the Mystery Machine."

Suddenly, a loud sound came from the room next door.

"Zoinks!" Shaggy cried.

**Chapter 3**

Susan led the gang to the next room. It was a recording studio. A teenage girl was reading a magazine. A teenage boy was tossing a tennis ball against the wall.

"That explains the noise," Velma said.

Susan introduced the gang to Andy and Mandy. They were the original Mystery Kids.

"Andy and Mandy, meet the

current owners of the Mystery Machine," Susan said.

Fred and Velma explained that strange things were happening with the van. Fred asked if they knew anything about the van.

"Well, it belonged to our keyboard player, Flash Flannigan," Susan said.

"Do you think we could talk to Flash?" Fred asked.

"Flash is in rock-and-roll heaven now," Susan said.

"Oh, man," Shaggy said. "The ghost of Flash Flannigan is haunting the Mystery Machine!"

As the gang left the house, they walked right into another teenager. He dropped a bunch of books on the ground.

"Who are you?" asked Daphne.

"I'm Randy," the boy said. "Andy and Mandy's brother."

Velma helped Randy pick up his books.

"Applied Science, sixth edition," she read. "Where do you study?"

"Defries Technical Academy," Randy said. "And I'm late for class!"

Randy grabbed his books and took off.

"That's strange," Daphne said. "Susan never mentioned that Andy and Mandy had a brother."

The gang thought about this as they walked. Soon, they were back in town.

"Like, we've got to find another way to get around," Shaggy said. "This walking is for the birds."

"Reah!" Scooby agreed.

Slowly and silently, the Mystery Machine rolled up next to them. The greenish glow caught their attention.

The gang ran down the street. The Mystery Machine was close behind them. But the street turned into a dead end!

"Hey, do you hear that?" asked Velma.

Eerie keyboard music filled the alley. The Mystery Machine began moving slowly toward the gang. It stopped about five feet from them. A loud noise came from its engine.

"Jinkies!" Velma exclaimed. "We're trapped!"

Chapter 4

"Got to think fast," Fred said.

Daphne took a box of Scooby
Snacks from her purse. She handed
it to Fred. Fred shook the box in
front of Scooby's face.

"A whole box, Scooby, all for you,"
Fred said. "Go get it!"

Fred tossed the box into the air.
Scooby leaped up. He grabbed the
box in his teeth. On his way down,
he caught hold of a fire escape lad-

der. The ladder lowered to the ground.

"Come on, everybody!" Fred called.

The gang scrambled up the ladder. The Mystery Machine sped up and slammed into the wall. It just missed the gang! A moment later, the van backed up and drove out of the alley.

"There's only one way to solve this mystery," Fred said. "Follow that van!"

The gang climbed down and ran back to the street. They started running after the van. Then they stopped in front of a red brick building.

"Defries Technical Academy,"

Velma said. "That's the school Randy Dinwiddie goes to. I wonder if he's there."

The gang went inside and found their way to the lab. Randy was there, working on some robot parts. The gang explained what had just happened with the Mystery Machine.

"Any idea why it would come to this school, Randy?" asked Fred.

"How should I know?" Randy said. "I never had anything to do with the Mystery Kids or their van. I'm just the tone-deaf brother."

"These robot arms are quite re-markable, Randy," Velma said. "But where are the controls?"

Randy pointed to his laptop computer. "With the wireless Internet, I don't need separate controls," he said. "I can make the robots do anything I want using my computer."

Randy typed on a few keys.

One of the robot arms began to move. It gave Scooby a pat on the head.

"Great work, Randy," Daphne said. "Your mother must be very proud of you."

"Yeah, right," Randy said. "She tries to help me with my homework. But I know she's just pretending to care. I'll never measure up to the Mystery Kids."

"Randy, what would you do if

your van started driving itself all over town?" Fred asked.

"I'd find myself a good mechanic," Randy said.

# Chapter 5

The gang decided to go back to Murph's. When they arrived, one of the garage doors was open.

"Murph? Yo, Murph!" Fred called.

Fred turned on a flashlight. Everyone looked around the garage.

"The van started acting funny after we got it back from Murph," Daphne said.

"Then he offered to buy it from us," Velma said. "I wonder why."

Fred's flashlight lit up a sign marked "Private." He slowly opened the door. Velma switched on the lights.

"Jeepers!" Daphne gasped as she looked around.

The whole room was covered with Mystery Kids posters, magazines, and pictures. Tables were piled with Mystery Kids action figures, lunch boxes, board games, night-lights, and other things.

"Whoa. Murph is a secret Mystery Kids fan," Daphne said.

There was a TV and VCR in the

corner of the room. Velma turned on the TV and pressed play.

The television program explained how Flash Flannigan disappeared after a concert one night. It also told how each week, a wild daisy appears on Flash's grave.

Velma turned off the television. "Sounds like weird things are happening at Flash Flannigan's grave," she said.

"Let's check it out!" Fred said.

"But how are we going to get there?" asked Daphne.

Fred shined his flashlight on some Mystery Kids stuff in the corner. Fred and Daphne chose the bicycle built for two. Velma grabbed a scooter, and Shaggy strapped on a pair of skates. Scooby jumped onto a skateboard.

At the graveyard, the gang saw Andy and Mandy standing by Flash's grave.

"What are they doing here?" wondered Daphne.

Andy and Mandy looked around, then walked away.

"Come on, gang," Fred said. "Let's follow them."

Suddenly, a greenish glow and spooky keyboard music filled the air. The Mystery Machine rose up over the hill behind them.

The gang split up. Fred and Daphne pedaled as fast as they could. Before the van could get them, they used a fallen headstone as a ramp. They sailed through the air and rode to safety.

Velma's scooter hit a bump. Her glasses flew off. Velma jumped off her scooter to look for them. But the Mystery Machine was heading straight for her! Just then, Scooby swooshed by on his skateboard. At the last minute, he saved Velma and her glasses.

Shaggy zipped down a wide path between the crypts. Suddenly, the Mystery Machine backed up right toward him! Its back doors were open. Shaggy tried to get away, but it was too late. He tumbled into the van. The doors shut behind him.

"The Mystery Machine's got Shaggy!" Velma exclaimed.

## Chapter 6

Fred and Daphne rode as fast as they could to catch up with the Mystery Machine. As Daphne pedaled, Fred climbed onto the handlebars. He leaped from the bike onto the back of the Mystery Machine.

"I'm coming, Shag," he called. "Hang in there! Whoa!"

The van zigzagged back and forth, trying to stop him. Inside the

van, Shaggy sat helplessly behind
the wheel.

"Whoa! Stop! Brake! Zoinnnnnks!"
he cried.

Fred climbed in through the window. He and Shaggy fought with
the steering wheel, but nothing
happened. Then they heard a
siren. A police car zoomed past and

cut off the van. The Mystery
Machine came to a sudden halt.

"Where'd you kids get your
licenses, clown school?" the policeman asked.

"We weren't driving, officer,"
Fred said.

"Come on, fella, that van can't
drive itself," the policeman said.

Daphne, Velma, and Scooby
finally caught up.

"You can believe him, officer!"
Daphne said. "The van has been
acting weird all week!"

The policeman decided to let the
gang go free. But he said the van
had to be locked up.

Another police car gave the gang

a ride to City Park. They found the stage where the Mystery Kids were practicing.

"Pick up the pace, kids," Susan called to them.

Mandy and Andy complained they needed a break.

"Complaining will only get you a one-way ticket to nowheresville," Susan said.

The gang went backstage and saw Randy on a ladder. He was hanging a large stage light.

"Like, we didn't think we'd see you here tonight," Shaggy said.

"My mom told me to set up a wireless lighting display," Randy said. "If I didn't, she said she'd stop paying for me to go to school."

Daphne watched the lights change colors over the stage.

"Jeepers! That's great!" Daphne said.

Susan heard Daphne's voice and walked over to the gang.

"Excuse me!" she said. "No one is allowed backstage!"

The gang walked down into the audience seats and saw Murph.

"We know why you're here," Daphne said.

"Yeah, I was looking for you," Murph said. "I saw your van on the news. So all I've got to say is . . . I'll give you $2,500. Take it or leave it."

Velma smiled. "And we know why you want it."

The gang told Murph that they saw his Mystery Kids collection. Murph admitted that he was a huge Mystery Kids fan. He wanted the Mystery Machine to complete his collection.

The music stopped suddenly. There was a crashing sound from backstage.

"Jinkies!" Velma exclaimed. "What was that?"

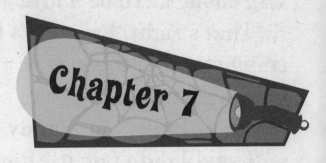

Chapter 7

The gang raced onto the stage.
Andy, Mandy, and Susan stood over
a broken stage light. It had fallen
from the light bar above the stage.

"Mom, Randy's trying to wreck
our show!" Mandy whined. "There
could've been a fire!"

Randy climbed down the ladder.

"No way, Mandy," Randy said.
"First, I wasn't even near that
light. And second, that's a fireproof

curtain. It's lined with lead. No way could there be a fire."

"That's right. I wouldn't let anything stand in the way of my babies' comeback," Susan said. "That includes you, Randy."

"I said I didn't do it!" Randy shouted.

"Then who did?" asked Daphne.

"Maybe it was the ghost of Flash Flannigan," Shaggy said.

"I doubt it," Velma said. "But that gives me an idea. Why don't we let Flash himself clear up this mystery?"

"How?" asked Fred.

"Daphne's going to hold a seance!" Velma said.

Daphne and Fred nodded at each

other. They ran backstage to get ready.

"Like, what's a seance? Is there food?" asked Shaggy.

"A seance is where you contact spirits from beyond the grave," Velma said.

"R-r-r-r-rave?" shuddered Scooby.

"So why don't you and Shaggy go help Daphne and Fred?" Velma said.

A few minutes later, Daphne called everyone backstage. She wore a long purple robe and sat at a round table draped with a green sheet.

"We are here to contact the spirit of Flash Flannigan," Daphne said in a mysterious voice. "I am the great Madame Daphne."

"Where did you learn to contact spirits?" asked Susan.

"On TV. Now watch this," Daphne said. "Spirits, make this table rise . . ."

To everyone's amazement, the table rose off the ground.

"Thank you, spirits," Daphne said.

"Rou're relcome," came a voice

from under the table. It sounded a lot like Scooby.

Daphne closed her eyes. "Everyone please join hands."

Daphne rocked back and forth. The table banged around. Daphne opened her eyes.

"Flash Flannigan is here," she said. "Flash, where are you?"

"Like, I'm deep in the ground," came another voice from under the table. It sounded a lot like Shaggy. "But I'm also in the air, and maybe even, like, the universe."

Daphne asked Flash who had taken over the Mystery Machine. Was it Andy and Mandy, wanting attention for the Mystery Kids? Was it Randy, to get back at his brother and sister? Or was it Murph, trying to get the gang to sell the van?

Before Flash could answer, the sound of eerie keyboard music filled the air. Everyone saw a greenish glow above the nearby hill.

"Wow! I'm good!" Daphne said.

The Mystery Machine drove over the hill. It headed straight for the stage.

"Run!" Fred called.

The Mystery Machine roared toward them. It zoomed up the steps and onto the stage. As it passed the curtain, Velma yanked a rope. The curtain fell and landed right on top of the van. The Mystery Machine came to a halt.

Chapter 8

Everyone came out from back-stage. They circled around the van.

"Like, it stopped," Shaggy said. "How come?"

"Because the lead-lined curtain is keeping wireless commands from getting through to its computers," Velma explained.

"And the person sending those commands is right over here!" Fred said. He walked over to the table

and pulled off the tablecloth. Susan sat under the table, holding a laptop computer.

"Mom!" exclaimed Andy, Mandy, and Randy.

"Susan wanted the Mystery Kids to be back on top of the music world," Velma said. "So she came up with this idea for the concert."

"That's why she helped you with your homework, Randy," Fred said. "So she could learn how to control the Mystery Machine by computer."

"Susan saw the Mystery Machine at Murph's," Velma said. "That's when she installed a computer inside the van."

"That meant she could control the Mystery Machine from anywhere," Fred said.

"But Susan had to make it seem like Flash Flannigan's ghost was controlling the van," Daphne said. "So she added a few extras." Daphne hit a key on the computer. The greenish glow filled the stage.

"Like, it's that scary greenish glow!" Shaggy said.

Fred kneeled down and pulled something out from under the van.

"Relax, Shaggy. They're just green Christmas lights," he said.

"My favorite clue was the eerie music that came from the van," Velma said. "It's the same sour note that came from Susan's piano. That means she must have recorded the music, not Flash Flannigan!"

"Speaking of Flash, what were you two doing at his grave?" asked Daphne.

"Flash was our hero. And our friend," Andy said. "We miss him."

"I never meant for the van to get so out of control," Susan said. "But you kids wouldn't stop meddling. It doesn't matter, though. The

Mystery Kids are still going to be bigger than ever!"

"Sorry, Mom, but the Mystery Kids are calling it quits," Andy said.

"Wait a minute," Mandy said, thinking. "I guess that light falling really was an accident."

"That's what I was trying to tell you!" Randy said.

"Sorry we were so hard on you, Randy," Mandy said. "From now on, all of us kids are going to stick together."

Susan watched in disbelief as her three children walked away, arm in arm.

"Kids! Wait for me!" she called. She ran after them.

The gang gathered around the Mystery Machine.

"It's good to have the good ol' Mystery Machine back on our side," Fred said.

Murph walked over. "$8,000, and that's my final offer," he said.

"It's not for sale, Murph!" the gang shouted together.

The next day, the gang fixed up the Mystery Machine. That night, they went to a drive-in movie. Before the show, they visited the snack bar.

"Like, what better way to celebrate getting the van back than taking it to the movies," Shaggy said.

As they walked, they heard the

eerie music again. The Mystery
Machine was following them — but
no one was driving!

"Zoinks!" Shaggy cried, dropping
his popcorn. "The Mystery Machine
is alive again!"

Scooby sat up from behind the
steering wheel. He had a big smile
on his face.

"Rooby-Dooby-Doo!" he cheered.